PUFFIN BOOKS
UK | USA | Canada | Ireland | Australia
India | New Zealand | South Africa

Puffin Books is part of the Penguin Random House group of companies
whose addresses can be found at global.penguinrandomhouse.com.

www.penguin.co.uk   www.puffin.co.uk   www.ladybird.co.uk

Penguin
Random House
UK

First published in Great Britain 2019
001

Printed in China
A CIP catalogue record for this book is available from the British Library

ISBN: 978–0–241–35505–3

All correspondence to:
Puffin Books
Penguin Random House Children's
80 Strand, London WC2R 0RL

PETER RABBIT™

I LOVE YOU, MUMMY

the WORLD is BIG

I
am
SMALL,

But
YOU
LIFT
me
UP

MAKE *me*

TALL.

Come RAIN or SHINE

BY *my* SIDE,

To
SHOW the
WAY

be MY GUIDE.

WHEN *I'm*
FEELING

A MUDDLE,

Your
LOVING
arms

give
ME
CUDDLE.

You
ALWAYS
KNOW

what
TO SAY,

and do **KIND** THINGS

for me
EACH
DAY.

So as I
GROW

and SPREAD my
WINGS,

I CAN'T
WAIT
to see

what
each DAY
BRINGS.

Thank
you
FOR
LOVING
me

like
YOU
DO,

and

DEAR
MUMMY,
I love

you
too.